Pete the Cat's

12
Groovy
Days
of
Christmas

Kimberly & James Dean

HARPER

An Imprint of HarperCollinsPublishers

ISBN 978-0-06-267527-9
The artist used pen and ink with watercolor and acrylic paint on
300lbs press paper to create the illustrations for this book.
Typography by Jeanne L. Hogle
19 20 SCP 10 9 8 7 6 5 4 3 2
❖
First Edition

On the first day of Christmas,
Pete gave to me . . .

a road trip to the sea.

GROOVY!

On the second day of Christmas,
Pete gave to me . . .

On the third day of Christmas,
Pete gave to me . . .

2 fuzzy gloves,
and a road trip to the sea.

GROOVY!

On the fourth day of Christmas,
Pete gave to me . . .

4 far-out surfboards,

On the fifth day of Christmas,
Pete gave to me . . .

5 ONION RINGS,

On the sixth day of Christmas,
Pete gave to me . . .

6 skateboards rolling,

5 ONION RINGS,
4 far-out surfboards,
3 yummy cupcakes,
2 fuzzy gloves,
and a road trip to the sea.

GROOVY!

On the seventh day of Christmas,
Pete gave to me . . .

7 concert tickets,

6 skateboards rolling,
5 ONION RINGS,
4 far-out surfboards,
3 yummy cupcakes,
2 fuzzy gloves,
and a road trip to the sea.

GROOVY!

On the eighth day of Christmas,
Pete gave to me . . .

On the ninth day of Christmas,
Pete gave to me . . .

On the tenth day of Christmas,
Pete gave to me . . .

10 sloths a-sleeping,

9 ugly sweaters,
8 guitars strumming,
7 concert tickets,
6 skateboards rolling,
5 ONION RINGS,
4 far-out surfboards,
3 yummy cupcakes,
2 fuzzy gloves,

and a road trip
to the sea.

GROOVY!

On the eleventh day of Christmas, Pete gave to me . . .

11 balls a-bouncing,

10 sloths a-sleeping,
9 ugly sweaters,
8 guitars strumming,
7 concert tickets,
6 skateboards rolling,

5 ONION RINGS,
4 far-out surfboards,
3 yummy cupcakes,
2 fuzzy gloves,

and a road trip
to the sea.

GROOVY!

On the twelfth day of Christmas,
Pete gave to me . . .

12 friends a-rockin',

11 balls a-bouncing,
10 sloths a-sleeping,
9 ugly sweaters,
8 guitars strumming,
7 concert tickets,
6 skateboards rolling,
5 ONION RINGS,
4 far-out surfboards,
3 yummy cupcakes,
2 fuzzy gloves,

. . . and a road trip to the sea.

GROOVY!